POTBELLY

°and the Haunted House°

ORCHARD BOOKS
96 Leonard Street, London EC2A 4RH
Orchard Books Australia
14 Mars Road, Lane Cove, NSW 2066
First published in Great Britain 1996
First paperback publication 1997
Text © Rose Impey 1996
Illustrations © Keith Brumpton 1996
A CIP catalogue record for this book is available
from the British Library.
1 85213 891 2 (hardback)
1 86039 388 8 (paperback)
Printed in Great Britain

POTBELLY

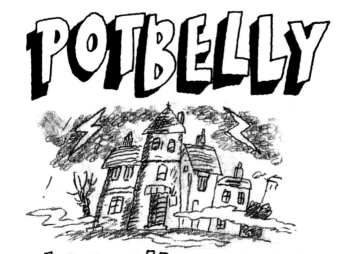

and the Haunted House

Rose Impey
Keith Brumpton

ORCHARD BOOKS

POTBELLY'S RAP

Number one is Potbelly,
because he's so big.
He's brave, he's clever;
he's a popular pig.
Peewee's the smallest,
and he's number two,
Because he's Potbelly's best pal,
his right-hand shrew.
Hi-Tech Turtle has his ear
to the ground.
He's a cool dude, he's laid back,
he's wired for sound.

Potbelly ↑

Peewee ↑

Hi-Tech

POTBELLY'S

Tough-Nut

Toughnut's a squirrel,
she's a hard nut to crack.
She does karate and kung fu
in case of attack.
But Lovestruck Lizard
isn't tough; he's shy.
He's a dreamer, he's a poet,
a real soft guy.
He's got two cousins,
who tag along too:
The Salamander Sisters,
when there's nothing else to do.

Lovestruck ↑

The Salamander Sisters

· My love is like
A red red ro
an

So it's business as usual,
they're all flat broke.
No money for a pizza,
a burger, or a coke.
They've nowhere to go
and nothing else to do,
but hang around the fish shop,
waiting for you.

Potbelly's bored.
The gang's bored too.
They're hanging round the fish shop
with nothing to do.

SNAPPER'S
Fish 'n chips

Snapper's Menu

Haddock . . . .
Cod . . . .
Plaice . . . .
Chicken. . . . .
Turkeyburger . . . .
½lb burger best BSE be
Egg Roll . . . .
Spring Roll . . . .
Sausage Roll . . . . . .
Rock n' Roll . . . . . .
Chips . . . .
Sausage . . . .
Bread and batter

cold nose

soul

zzz

Snapper's on the war-path,
listen to him shout,
"I don't want you lot on my step.
Find a new hang-out."

danger of
being
battered !!

Snapper

"Snapper in a
more friendly
mood

So Potbelly tells them,
"A den is what we need.
A secret hide-out of our own."
They vote; it's all agreed.

Hi-Tech knows a house,
it's not far away.
The trouble is it's haunted,
or that's what people say.

"Don't care," says Toughnut.
"Doesn't bother me.
Don't believe in ghosts and things.
Don't scare easily."

"Yeah," says Potbelly.
"We're not mardy-bums.
We're not scared of ghosts and things.
We don't care what comes."

"So let's go," says Peewee.
The gang starts to walk.
The Salamander Sisters say,
"You lot, you're all talk."

The house looks scary,
it's dark and it's old,
the kind of house in horror films
that makes your blood run cold.

But Potbelly's boss,
he's leader, after all.
So he puts on a brave face
and climbs up the wall.

The door's unlocked.
They go in one by one.
"Boy, this is great," says Toughnut,
"we can have some fun."

It's creepy inside.
It doesn't feel like fun.
The gang aren't happy,
they wish they hadn't come.

But they try to look brave,
they don't make a fuss.
The Salamander Sisters say,
"You're not fooling us."

In case someone comes,
Hi-Tech stands on guard.
The others sit round on the floor,
they play a game of cards.

Suddenly they hear
some creaks and a groan
coming from the upstairs room.
They want to go home!

It sounds like a ghost,
perhaps a monster too.
They can't concentrate on cards,
they don't know what to do.

"Don't care," says Toughnut.
"Doesn't bother me.
Don't believe in ghosts and things.
Don't scare easily."

"That's right," says Potbelly.
"We're not scaredy-cats.
We don't believe in ghosts and things.
It's probably just rats."

The noise gets louder.
They creep up one by one.
The Salamander Sisters say,
"These rats must weigh a ton."

They're outside the door,
what will they find?
Will there be a monster
or a ghost inside?

"Don't care," says Toughnut.
"Doesn't bother me.
Don't believe in ghosts and things.
Don't scare easily."

"That's r-r-right," says Potbelly.
"We're made of s-s-strong stuff.
We don't believe in ghosts and things.
We're r-r-really t-t-tough."

The door swings open.
Potbelly sees red.
There's Fang, his biggest enemy,
jumping on the bed.

It was Fang and his gang
making all that din.
"It's our den," says Potbelly
"Who let you lot in?"

"It's our den," says Fang.
He looks fit to burst.
"Go and find a den of your own.
We found this place first."

Everyone's angry,
they're ready to fight
when they hear Hi-Tech whistle.
Someone's come in sight.

It's old Sergeant Snout,
he's walking his beat.
He sees something suspicious;
he comes across the street.

"I know you're in there.
You'd better all come out,
or I'm coming in after you,"
calls old Sergeant Snout.

"Don't care," says Toughnut.
"Doesn't bother me.
Don't care about Sergeant Snout.
Don't scare easily."

"I don't care," says Fang.
"Let old Snout come in."
"And I don't care," says Potbelly.
They both start to grin.

Then they hear footsteps
coming up the stairs.
Suddenly they're not so brave,
now they all feel scared.

In less than a second
everyone's gone.
They've all found a place to hide,
all of them but one.

Poor old Potbelly,
he's too big to hide.
He can't fit in anywhere,
he's far too wide.

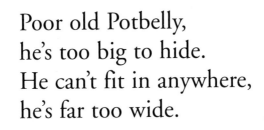

He's caught red-handed
by old Sergeant Snout.
He takes him to the station.
"Now what's all this about?"

But Potbelly's brave,
he takes all the blame.
He says he won't give Sergeant Snout
anybody's name.

The gang's very lucky
this pig didn't squeal.

Cash for
Potbelly's meal

Recei~~xxxxx~~eived

PeeWee £1

Tough £1

Lovestruck £5

Hi-tech £1-50

Salamander Sisters ~~owe~~ owe
50p each

They share out their pocket money
and treat him to a meal.

Potbelly's happy,
he's got lots to eat.
He thinks it's worth getting caught
for this kind of feast.

Scary!
Next the sheep crept in and picked it up. But the voice said, I'm the ghost of Auntie Mabel that £10 note stays on the table. The sheep ran off bleating.
I don't blame him.
So the horse crept in and picked it up. But when the voice said, I'm the ghost of Auntie Mabel That £10 note stays on the table, the horse said, I'm the ghost of Davy Crockett This £10 note goes in my pocket. And he ran off with it.
That's a smart horse!
the end

You can read more about Potbelly
in these other books...

Potbelly in Love

185213 894 7 (hb)   1 86039 391 8 (pb)

Potbelly's Lost His Bike

1 85213 892 0 (hb)   1 86039 389 6 (pb)

Potbelly Needs a Job

1 85213 893 9 (hb)   1 8 6039 390 X (pb)